yo-ni-korn

Andy Blood

COUNTERFEIT
BOOKS LTD

To all yoo-ni-korns past, present and future,
but especially mine: India and Zac.

First published by Counterfeit Books Limited, 27/59 Sackville Street, Grey Lynn,
Auckland 1021, New Zealand.

A catalogue record for this book is available from the National Library of New
Zealand.

ISBN 978-1-9911975-1-1 (Softcover - POD)

Cover concept by Andy Blood.
Cover design by Nic Neame.
Internal design and typography by Cheryl Smith.

Contents

Introduction

Unicorn *yoo-ni-korn*
Collective noun: *a blessing of unicorns*

Which raises the question: Is it a blessing to be born a unicorn?

It's a little-known fact that one in a billion people is born a unicorn. It happens entirely at random, and a unicorn is just as likely to be born into a family that lives in a slum, a tenement or a project as they are to be born into a privileged middle-class family.

We can't be certain — because the family will often go to great lengths to hide their precious baby unicorn — but right now, there are probably about half a dozen real live unicorns on the planet.

Here's how to spot one:

1   *Rainbows:* Unicorns attract rainbows like flowers attract bees. So, if someone has an above-average quota of rainbows in their selfies, that could be a sign.

2   *Vomit:* Unicorn vomit is not like your vomit, or mine — a unicorn's vomitus contains every colour of the rainbow. While on a good day (well, bad day to be honest), you and I might find carrots in our vom, a unicorn might discover a veritable vegetal smorgasbord in theirs — red (pepper), orange (peel or carrots), yellow (sweetcorn), green (broccoli or pepper), blue (berries), indigo (plums) and even violet (purple cabbage).

3   *A horn:* Funnily enough, the trait that you would think is the most telltale of all is often the one you are least likely to spot. And that's because parents of a baby unicorn will — via surgery, hairstyle or headgear — attempt to remove or disguise the evidence that their offspring has a horn.

4   *A mane:* Long, lustrous locks — easily chopped or disguised.

5   *A tail:* Easily covered or hidden.

6   *Skin coloration:* An iridescent sheen that in the right light sparkles with blues, lavenders and purples. (Sometimes mistaken for bruising.)

The following stories are those of the six living creatures who are half-human, half-unicorn. It would be naïve to think all such births are welcomed and celebrated.

In fact, they're not fairy tales at all.

Cast

Navi (she/her)(they/them)
Khukhkhuu (he/him)
Bai Longma (he/him)
Tuyana-Solongo (she/her)(they/them)
Baby Y (not given)
Baby Z (not given)

The Narwhal

*The narwhal, also known as 'the unicorn of the sea',
is a medium-sized toothed whale which lives in the
Arctic waters around Greenland, Canada and Russia.
A narwhal is distinguished by a long, straight, helical
tusk which can measure up to 2 metres long. They're
hunted by indigenous communities in Greenland
and Canada for local consumption and to sustain a
lucrative international market for their tusks.*

THIS STORY TAKES PLACE IN GREENLAND.

When the baby was born everyone cried. She was one of those special ones. Those often talked about in hushed tones, but rarely seen in human form. She was quickly wrapped in swaddling clothes, with special care being taken to cover her crown. If word got out, there would be trouble. A story was hatched: an assisted birth had required the midwife to use a ventouse, which had elongated the baby's forehead. And that was the last anyone in Disko Bugten (Disko Bay) heard of the matter. But for little Navi, it was only the beginning of her unusual life.

At first it wasn't a problem — the wearing of hats being commonplace at preschool. But as the kids began to explore active play, little Navi found herself having to avoid games such as football, where heading the ball would be a challenge. There were upsides. Fancy dress parties were fun, for example, and a chance to play with her 'gift' in unusual ways. A chance to be her real self. A chance for a real unicorn to hide in plain sight. Likewise, Halloween. But in truth the barely-there appendage wouldn't come into its own until later.

It was with puberty that things really changed. Everyone in class developed something or other: bumps, hairs, height, deeper voices. Little Navi, however, developed bumps like the rest of the girls and an appendage not unlike the boys, which became increasingly hard to hide. Her peers became spiteful, and the name-calling more hurtful. Cock-head, hornbag, kid-rhino … You get the picture. She began to feel ostracised. And embarrassment about her appearance meant she was increasingly homebound. Yet even her safe haven was presenting its own set of problems — the height of the average doorway wasn't prepared with unicorns in mind, for example — and she began to retreat from the world. And all the while her horn grew and grew.

But even when she withdrew, she was not left alone.

Rumour was rife that there was a price on her head, both literally and figuratively. A photo of her would fetch thousands; and if it showed her unicorn horn in all its glory, tens of thousands. So she was stalked. Her privacy invaded. Drones buzzed her home. Journalists rifled through her garbage. Former friends told tales. On the really bad days she considered ending it all. Even on the manageable days she dreamed of removing the horn by one means or another. She even tried to find a surgeon who would operate but in Nuuk no such surgeons existed. She would have to fly to Denmark to receive medical treatment of that sort and that was out of the question. So she felt she had no other choice but to go dark. She disappeared herself.

And soon the people of Disko Bugten turned their attention to other matters. They had other unicorns to hunt. Those of the sea. With summer fading and fall approaching, the time of the annual narwhal harvest had arrived.

Her people still ate whale meat, and the skin and blubber (known as *mattak*) which was considered by some to be a delicacy. With a few even adding it to coffee as a replacement for sugar, so the fat melts in the coffee. Weird? It takes all sorts. But with retail prices for *mattak* having risen by almost a thousand-fold in the past few decades, the harvest had never been more lucrative and more welcome. An illicit few also seized the chance to harvest the ivory tusks and feed collectors' appetites for this exotic appendage.

The Greenlanders would venture out in small boats and in kayaks, harpoon the whales, and finish them off with a carefully aimed rifle shot. Perhaps a hundred narwhal would be culled this way each season.

Further north, Navi was living in a small cabin (albeit one with suitably customised high doorways). With her haven being infused by the light of the aurora borealis — a shimmering night-time rainbow — few would disagree that living under such a spectral display was a fitting place for a half-human half-unicorn to be.

But as much as Navi tried to cut herself off from events back home, the other electronic displays in her cabin were filled with electrically charged images of their own: those of the annual narwhal harvest. And she couldn't put the carnage out of her mind. A species with a horn just like hers — they were practically related — was being hunted for a trophy; a horn just like her own. She pictured her own head mounted on a trophy wall someday, horn resplendent, an unknown collector standing proudly in front regaling a coterie of friends with how they came by such a prize.

She shuddered. If not me, them. She couldn't just sit by in splendid isolation and watch. She would have to do something about it. She would have to come out.

Not long after, interest in the narwhal cull exploded. An unusual creature —half-human and half-narwhal — had been seen swimming amongst the pods of whales and thus spoiling the hunt. The indigenous fisherman, like fishermen the world over, were a superstitious lot and had been well and truly spooked. For this mysterious aquatic creature (unlike the narwhals) had long hair, which reminded many of the old Greenlandic myth of the Mother of the Sea, whose trademark was her long, flowing tresses.

They began urgent whispered discussions about what this omen portended, finally agreeing that the Mother of Sea had sent the creature to warn them: nature was hurting. And so, just as the myth demanded, the fishermen began to throw their harpoons into the sea. The harvest was put on ice.

Then when the aquatic chimera pulled itself from the water revealing its neoprene skin, scuba-diving tanks and glorious metre-long horn, the world's jaw dropped. Navi lifted her scuba mask to reveal it was her. And the following moment — when she pulled entangled crustacea from her hair — will forever be enshrined in Greenlandic popular lore. For in the Greenlandic myth, when the Mother of the Sea's hair is cleaned of all its accumulated detritus, it is a sign that balance had been restored. And Navi had, to all intents and purposes, done exactly that — in front of the world's media.

To non-Greenlanders, however, and to the world's media in particular, she was the catch of the decade. A half-human, half-unicorn creature more valuable than a thousand narwhal tusks, and whose neoprene *mattak* made a huge splash all over TikTok. Now her unicorn horn — once an impediment — was celebrated the world over without ever being a trophy on a wall.

All the moment needed was a rainbow to form in the sky and the image would be complete.

And in many people's minds, it did.

Little Blue

*Set between Ulaanbaatar and Karakorum
(Kharkhorin), once the capital of the Mongol empire.
And south of Lake Khövsgöl, the 'younger sister' of Lake
Baikal and the second most voluminous freshwater lake
in Asia. Sometimes known as 'Ocean Khövsgöl' ('Ocean
Mother') or Khövsgöl nuur. It is a sacred place.*

THIS STORY TAKES PLACE IN MONGOLIA.

According to some Eastern traditions, when a baby
doesn't want to leave the womb the Goddess of Baby
Sending kicks it out. And it is this encouragement
from on high that accounts for the blue bruise often
seen on the lower backs of Asian babies, which many
call the 'Mongolian blue spot'.

The child in our story, though, was born with more
than a standard-issue blue bruise. Indeed the iridescent
blue-indigo-violet sheen on its lower back led some to
suggest that a unicorn had done the kicking out. And
if the colouring alone wasn't evidence enough, the

protuberance on the baby's forehead was conclusive. And so – regardless of whether the propulsive nudge did come courtesy of the goddess's toe rather than a unicorn's hoof – the distinctive bruise our babe, little Khukhkhuu (meaning 'blue boy'), entered this world sporting would lead some to call him the Uni-Khan, and others, our little blue boy.

This kind of birth had happened before, of course, when the Earth was young, but that was a long, long time ago. For the tribes peopling Mongolia had been among the first on Earth to tame wild horses, and the two species had co-existed for thousands of years. Their affinity with wild horses had indeed become the stuff of legends. And so, as we gallop forward to little Khukhkhuu's arrival, Mongolia would seem an ideal location if any heavenly footwork were to take place. Indeed, one popular reading of the current situation was that the gods had sent this special child as a means of honouring the partnership between horse and man.

Now if there is one thing the good people of Mongolia like almost as much as horses, it is making merry. So the auspicious birth duly became a cause for much celebration, with the kinsfolk hurriedly preparing a feast. A lamb was slaughtered for the occasion, before being roasted on a spit, and consumed nose to tail. The birth was toasted with *airag* – fermented mare's milk – also known as *kumis*, and sometimes referred to as *cosmos*. Fitting then, that under the stars, they toasted the real cosmos itself for this special blessing.

And it seems the cosmos was in a mood to return the compliment. For as they raised their tankards in thanks, shooting stars passed overhead, bursting into flame as they entered the atmosphere. The whole tribe was intoxicated with joy, and fireworks lit up the night.

Mongolian children are raised on horseback and are expected to be accomplished riders by the age of three, and little Khukhkhuu would prove no exception. Horse mastery was a prerequisite for the tribe, and he excelled at it. In a nod to his evident equine connection, his family grew his hair long and were only too happy to accentuate its mane-like quality. The little 'Uni-Khan' was becoming their means to greater status. For it was not just his hair that was growing; so, too, was his horn.

As word spread of this boy marvel, people began to make pilgrimages just to touch his horn, as if merely doing so extended a blessing. Couples wanting to conceive would ask him to bless their union. Those carrying unborn children would ask him to lay his horn across their pregnant bellies. At first, while young, little Khukhkhuu was compliant if a little bemused with the demands made of him, but as he grew older he became frustrated with the fuss, and was increasingly inclined to leave such human foibles behind. The community might venerate him and hold him close, but he was finding the continual attention cloying and claustrophobic. He spent more and more time on horseback, and would disappear for days at a time. The call of the wild was strong.

The vastness of the steppes was his domain. And there he was free. For there, no one batted an eyelid at his unusual appearance. No one intruded into his space to beg a favour. No one fawned over him, grabbed at him, called him their Uni-Khan or 'little blue boy' in breathless tones. No one. Just himself and his horses, the winds and the wilds. Over time, the frequency of his absences increased, and the time spent away lengthened. Until one day he didn't return.

His people were bereft. Surely their magic boy would not have willingly chosen to leave his people? Some misfortune must have befallen him. Had he been thrown from his horse? Had he fallen prey to a pack of wolves? Or crossed paths with a wandering band of ne'er-do-wells? Perhaps he'd been spirited away and across the border into either Russia or China? Nobody knew. All the people of the vast empty steppes did know was that they felt emptier, and less blessed, for the departure of their Uni-Khorn. For he was never seen again.

Zhangye

A list of the best places to view rainbows often includes the island of Kaua'i (Hawai'i being known as the rainbow state), the Niagara Falls (Canada–United States), the Victoria Falls (Zambia) and the Iguazú Falls (Brazil/Argentina), Yosemite (Sierra Nevada, United States; and equally famous for its moonbows — when the light of the moon is refracted through the waterfall's mist), the Cumberland Falls (Kentucky, United States), The Rockies (Canada–United States), Lake Neusiedl (Austria), and the west coast of Ireland, the misty Emerald Isle.

Equally breathtaking, and formed in an entirely different manner, however, are the Rainbow Mountains of China (near Zhangye city), where striped sedimentary layers of sandstone, iron and trace minerals form the same spectacular spectrum of colours that we normally see in the sky. Only these are a permanent fixture, having been created in stone 24 million years ago. And, strangely, these rainbows are best seen without any rainfall at all.

THIS STORY TAKES PLACE NEAR ZHANGYE.

Bai Longma (named after the Chinese legend of the White Dragon Horse) was born in the shadow of the Rainbow Mountains near Zhangye, in the Gansu province of China. From birth he was as strong as a horse. And because of this, it was often said that he might one day carry the hopes and dreams of his people.

With the region's climate being so arid, many of the caves in the area have been used to store artefacts of all kinds for centuries, with some of the mummified relics being over two thousand years old.

Its inhospitable climate did not consign it to simply being a lock-up for treasures, though.

To the contrary, since time immemorial, its position as an outpost on the Silk Road (a caravan route linking east Asia with the Mediterranean) has meant that traders from myriad cultures, East and West, have passed through Zhangye. And, in doing so, they did not hurry past, anxiously covering the miles between one watering hole and the next. No, they tarried, enthralled by the iridescent silica on every mountainside, and paid their respects to the many deities and gods represented by the paintings, drawings and sculptures preserved in the caves.

And not everyone was passing through. There were local peoples who took great pride and responsibility in caring for the treasures stowed in their caves for safekeeping. Bai Longma was of these people. And so, for as long as young Bai Longma could remember, the caves were his playground. He knew many of the paintings and their stories, and was particularly drawn to those of his namesake, for there were many renderings of leaping, flying and shape-shifting white horses. Though it must be said, they were only small in number compared to the trove of more than 40,000 artworks in the caves.

To some, however, the vision of a galloping white horse set against a rainbow mountain backdrop conjures up one thing in particular: a unicorn. Given this, all Bai Longma needed was a spiralling horn and he would complete this magical pastoral evocation.

Now it must be noted that this powerful mystical linking of white steeds and rainbows was not the province of the Rainbow Mountains; though it had long existed in the imaginations and the cultural baggage — both figurative and literal — of the many peoples who traversed the Silk Road. So, it's not too much of a stretch to conjecture that the canny traders who plied their trade along the silk route saw opportunities to make some coin by adding wares depicting such enchanting visions to their caravan stock. This would certainly explain how the unicorns that had appeared in Greco-Roman frescoes since the Middle Ages came to grace palaces in the East, while Eastern artworks, carpets and antiquities came to decorate palaces in the West. Indeed, as far back as the sixth century BCE, unicorn mosaics were a feature in the palace of Apadana, in Susa, Iran. Tapestries reproducing such images were highly prized, and some even made their way as far as Stirling, in Scotland, to warm the walls of cold Caledonian castles.

But the allure of the unicorn was not confined just to décor and high art. It was widely rumoured that 'alicorn' — the substance that made up the horn — held magical and medicinal properties. As such, trade in alicorn — or whatever substance was a likely substitute for it — was brisk. It was regarded as being in the same rarefied category as ambergris (those various-sized lumps of a waxy flammable material supposedly produced in the stomach of sperm whales, so highly valued by perfume makers) and other such rarities as the hair, fingernails and toenails of saints.

And so, it was unknown to almost everyone in Zhangye (including Bai Longma himself) that there could well be a real live unicorn living in their midst, for Bai Longma had in fact been born with such a lump on his forehead. Upon seeing it at the boy's birth and fearing what this might mean for the young babe's future and longevity, the startled midwife had reported her discovery to a physician, who had swiftly removed the offending growth. All concerned were sworn to secrecy for the boy's sake; the only vestige remaining, his name: White Dragon Horse, which while it had its origins in the Chinese story 'Journey to the West' had become co-mingled with that of the near Eastern unicorn. Then, as Bai Longma had grown, the resulting not-insignificant scarring had gradually receded to his crown where it became covered in thick hair.

(In *Saiyuki*, a Japanese anime manga retelling of 'Journey to the West', the character of White Dragon Horse is played by 'Jeep', so named because he had the strength to ferry his companions throughout their epic quest, proving the Chinese story itself also had both the legs and stamina to travel far and wide. But I digress.)

The horn and its speedy removal were such a closely guarded secret that it had never, ever been mentioned even to Bai Longma. That is until one day, when his *lao ye* (grandfather) was on his deathbed and chose that moment to unburden his conscience and share with his grandson the secret of his birth that had hitherto been kept from him. To Bai Longma, this was like the proverbial lamplight coming on. The missing piece of a mosaic falling into place. His strength and size had always marked him out as exceptional but with this answer to his long-held sense of difference came a slew of further questions, which no one seemed able, or willing, to answer. He figured there was one person who could not feign ignorance. And so it was that he set his mind on one task: he would find the physician.

In Zhangye, physicians were few and far between, and so it didn't take long to locate the 'sawbones' concerned. Somewhat unfortunately perhaps in this instance, because the location in question was a burial plot, the physician having long since shuffled off this mortal coil.

The physician's next of kin was his daughter, Caihong, who lived locally. Bai Longma promptly called upon her and did his best to question her about his tale while at the same time trying not to appear too *sha* (crazy). Her response intrigued him further, because rather than cast aspersions on his sanity, the young woman simply said: 'My father always said that one day a young man would come and ask about his crown ...' She went further: 'To be honest, when he said this, I thought the old man was a little *sha* in the head himself. But if ever such a young man *were* to present himself, I was to give him this ...' And she went and fetched an envelope, which she passed to Bai Longma. Inside the envelope was a piece of desiccated parchment bearing a simple if somewhat cryptic message: *By a pomegranate tree ringed by a fence in a field of flowers, you will find your answer.*

They looked at each other blankly. Bai Longma decided to head home to have a think. And to meditate on this riddle. But his quiet reflection was soon interrupted by a loud, insistent banging at the door. And when he opened it, he was surprised to find the culprit was none other than Caihong, the physician's daughter.

'I have it!' she exclaimed. 'I have the answer. Follow me: we're going to the caves ...'

They hightailed it to Mogao Caves, and along the way she filled in the gaps in the story. She had researched the sentence written on the parchment and found that it described a tapestry — popular in the Middle Ages — of which supposedly there was a painting in the caves. The tapestry was called 'The Unicorn in Captivity', and portrayed just such a creature, which was chained to a pomegranate tree surrounded by a fence in a field of flowers. Apparently, a fair maiden had used her charms to lure the unicorn to the spot, whereupon it had been captured and chained to the tree. An early form of entrapment, you might say. If they could find the painting, it might help them find an answer, just as her father had predicted.

Bai Longma and Caihong's initial excitement quickly dimmed. While the link to the painting might be clear, the path to it was less so. For at Mogao there are hundreds of caves containing thousands of paintings, sculptures, mosaics, relics and artefacts. Still, any saga requires grit of its heroes, and so our pair resigned themselves to the difficult task ahead. Fortunately — this time thanks to the grit and fortitude of generations of local monks — the caves had been divided into five 'levels' according to age, which now at least gave Bai Longma and Caihong a starting point. Throughout the ages, as more and more treasures were brought to the caves, local monks had fastidiously brought order to impending chaos by sorting, cataloguing and arranging all the artefacts according to era. So, what could have been akin to finding a needle in a haystack was now more like finding a pin in a small matchbox.

That 'small matchbox' would be the caves containing

treasure from the era most closely correlated to the 16th century. While this narrowed the focus of their attention, there was still a trove to work their way through, but after a few hours hunting high and low, they found exactly what they were looking for. A cracked and peeling painted version of the exact scene described in the physician's parchment.

Now standing in front of the very thing they'd been searching for, they were once again perplexed. 'So, what now?' They looked at one another, then at the painting, then back at one another again. And the same thought passed through each of their minds: what on earth were they doing chasing unicorns? It was like chasing rainbows. Aware now of their fool's errand, Bai Longma dropped his gaze with embarrassment. And it was then that, for the very first time, he noticed the chain around Caihong's neck, on the end of which was a small tusk. Following the direction of his gaze, she explained: 'It was a gift from my father, given to me on his deathbed. He claimed it had magical powers.'

Bai Longma reached over and gently cradled the pendant. While he inspected the tusk-like object, she in turn lightly caressed his hairline, her fingers delicately parting his hair to reveal the birthmark on his crown. Simultaneously, a picture formed in both their minds. Perhaps the artefact dangling on the chain wasn't a tusk at all? Perhaps it was baby Bai Longma's fabled horn? And, just like the allegory in the picture, this unicorn had been lured to the scene by a young maiden. Again, there was form for this theory, for both Marco Polo and Leonardo da Vinci had been convinced that you needed a virgin to trap a unicorn.

And maybe that's what had happened here — or perhaps it's all just a load of old hokum. Still, for centuries the Silk Road has been the lodestar of trading in dreams and visions, and so Bai Longma and Caihong's tale slotted right in. Their story soon spread, and did wonders for the city, bringing many tourists to the area surrounding Rainbow Mountains. Which meant that, in a strange way, the prophecy about Bai Longma carrying the hopes and dreams of the people of the town on his shoulders came true.

And what lay in store for White Dragon Horse himself? Well, the pomegranate tree in the painting represents fertility, which is probably something that escaped the notice of our protagonists as they sat each sipping a cool glass of pomegranate juice in a nearby café. But it wasn't too long before Bai Longma and Caihong became an item, and soon after that got married. And nine months on, the land of the permanent rainbow was blessed with the patter of tiny (hoofed) feet.

So now, from whichever standpoint you looked at it, culturally speaking, the circle was complete. White Dragon Horse has found his Princess, which satisfies the Chinese myth. And the unicorn now has both his horn and his rainbow (Caihong meaning rainbow in Chinese) satisfying the Indo-European myth too. And so it was a double-happy ending.

The Pearl of Siberia

At 25-30 million years of age, Lake Baikal is the oldest freshwater lake on Earth. With a maximum recorded depth of 5387 feet (1642 metres), it is also the deepest. So deep, in fact, that fissures in the Earth's crust produce hot mineral springs in it. Containing about one-fifth of the world's freshwater, it's also teeming with life, and of the 2500 plant and animal species that live there, two-thirds do not live anywhere else on the planet. Species such as the nerpa, the world's only freshwater seal. It is little wonder, then, that Lake Baikal is called the Pearl of Siberia.

THIS STORY TAKES PLACE NEAR LAKE BAIKAL,
IN SIBERIA.

Was she a stallion or a mare? It was a question that often-crossed Tuyana's mind. It wasn't so much that she felt uncomfortable in her body or undecided about her identity — she felt very comfortable — but more that she didn't have the language to describe who she was or how it felt. It wasn't as simple as a binary choice between one or the other.

And it was true that, for the most part, people let her be. Some came sniffing around because of her very *other*ness, and indeed, some tried to date her for that very reason: hoping to bed her just to find out what it was like to sleep with someone who was half-unicorn. And it wasn't just boys either; girls were just as curious too. But as it transpired, she was just another one-of-a-kind species unique to Lake Baikal. Another one of Siberia's iridescent pearls. Not for nothing had she been given the Buryat name Tuyana-Solongo — Radiant Rainbow.

And Tuyana certainly felt very at home by the lake. In summer, she swam in it. In winter, when the ice was so thick you could walk on it, she rode a horse on it. Of course, this was a cause for great wonderment for any traveller seated on the Trans-Siberian Express who just happened to be looking out of the window at the exact moment the train wound its way around the lake. A mounted unicorn traversing the ice undoubtedly adding to the mystique of their journey.

Freight trains, too, would circumnavigate the lake at a crawl, and their dogged, steady progress would sometimes prove a temptation Tuyana found herself powerless to resist. When this happened, she would find herself train-hopping and riding the train to nearby Ulan-Ude, where she would cast off her usual solitude and spend a night carousing with friends.

Ulan-Ude's position at the edge of the Russian Far East (5642 kilometres from Moscow) means it is the place where Russian classicism and Buddhism first intermingled, married, and had children. Proof that it had been settled by both Cossacks and Buryati Mongols is evident everywhere in the city — which was inaccessible to foreigners until the late 1980s — as it features both pagodas and orthodox onion-domed spires. Rather unusually, perhaps, it also boasts the world's largest sculpture of Lenin's head. Weighing more than 40 tonnes and towering more than 7 metres high, its sheer size means Lenin's constructivist frown is visible all over the city. There's simply no avoiding it.

And there is something else the inhabitants of the region can't avoid. Something more potent than the powers mentioned above. Something older and deeper. Something that seeps into every pore of everyday life: shamanism, which includes paying respect to other-than-human deities through sacrifice.

The events following one such freight-hopping occasion unfolded in such a way that they were destined to go down in popular lore. Tuyana had gone into the city to catch up with friends, which involved consuming copious amounts of the local libation *tarasun*, also known as 'milk whisky', washed down with shots of the local vodka Rodniki Sibiri (Springs of Siberia). Before long the usual well-oiled hijinks ensued: card games, karaoke and Buryati ethnic dancing. An eyewitness account (surfaced from police testimony) gives some

29

colour to the evening's events "... *when the Buryat girls are slightly drunk and start dancing you see the greatness of the steppe, how slender trees bend in the wind. You see how the sun rises and Baikal sparkles ...*" to which a less than generous witness added: "... *but some were dancing like nerpas ...*"

Libidos were lit, with the males and females putting on displays for one another. Teasing, flirting and testing each other's boundaries — and the boundaries of what was permissible. All under the baleful glare of Lenin. Their bald-faced cheek, his bald-faced head.

On they partied into the wee small hours, until they finally crashed — as they so often did — in one another's arms.

And while our merry-makers slept, the rest of the city awoke to find a new addition to Ulan-Ude's skyline. A red-and-white-striped road cone now took pride of place smack-centre on Lenin's forehead, transforming him into a unicorn of massive proportions. The inventive relocation of the ubiquitous red-and-white road cone from roadworks to high-brow altar — the universal symbol of 'a great night out' — caught everyone's eye, including that of the local guard. Like Lenin, they were not amused.

It didn't take the authorities long to identify their culprit. After all, a party of drunken revellers — one of whom was themselves a unicorn — was hardly inconspicuous, and multiple witnesses were pointing the officers of the law in the same direction. So it was that Tuyana was fingered for the daring deed and found herself remanded in jail before appearing in front of the local *magistrat*. When the time came to face the consequences, Ulan-Ude's worthy dispenser of justice promptly sentenced her to 100 hours of community service, to be spent polishing the dome of Lenin's head.

This time, there was no need for our somewhat dusty rainbow to train-hop her way home: this time she was escorted back from Ulan-Ude in the rear of a Russian police force Skoda Octavia. Handcuffed and jammed between two stone-faced police officers who clearly thought it was important that police procedure was followed to the letter. It was a long ride, with headaches all round. Nevertheless, the two rigid upholders of the law proved only too happy to pose for a photograph with Tuyana when they released her on the shores of Lake Baikal.

"Was she a stallion or a mare?" She was a nightmare, they concluded. Albeit a radiant one.

Footnote:

*The name Baikal might have derived from the Yakut words bye «rich», kel «lake», i.e. rich lake. Many linguists believe that the name came from the Turkic-Mongolian «Baigal», which means «big body of water», or from the Chinese Bai-Hai, which means «north sea». The Buryats called it Baigal-Nuur «Lake Baikal». A definitive answer to this question has not yet been found.

This information is taken from the following source: Berkin N. S. Baikal studies: textbook / N. S. Berkin, A. A. Makarov, O. T. Rusinek. - Irkutsk: Publishing house of Irkutsk State University, 2009. - P. 8

Double Rainbow

All context and background to this story is Classified.

THIS STORY TAKES PLACE IN **REDACTED**.

While a live unicorn birth is clearly very special — being a one-in-a-billion-people event — even more remarkable must be the birth of unicorn twins. As with their human counterparts, unicorn twins can be either fraternal or identical, the latter being even more rare. Relying as it does on the splitting of a unicorn zygote at the exact moment of conception to create two genetically identical unicorn beings, this exceedingly rare occurrence — a double blessing, as it were — is known among the cognoscenti as a 'double rainbow'.

In the grand scheme of things — statistics and large numbers being what they are — there is no reason on Earth why a blessing so remarkable should be bestowed only on people whom we already regard as 'special', whether that status is conferred by wealth, privilege, class, or some other bias-ridden construct. Which means there's no need, in our pursuit of unicorn twins, to focus our search on places where these already privileged souls congregate — be that London, Paris, New York or, for that matter, Shanghai. No, that would be too neat. Probability decrees that this event could take place anywhere, at any time, and could happen to anyone – such as Mother X (whose name has been withheld here for reasons of privacy).

And so it was that, casting our gaze wide, we were eventually rewarded when our eye fell on a small hospital where just such a miracle event was unfolding. And the miracle was about to provide another unforeseen twist ...

The actual process of giving birth is often described as like passing a bowling ball. In this case then, a more apt description might be like passing two bowling balls, each with a ten-pin bowling pin attached on top. 'Ouch,' you might say. Now, as with many multiple births, a C-section had been advised in the interests of both safety and comfort. And the decision for surgical intervention here proved fortuitous, as those present for the birth would no doubt have concurred. Because it was soon evident that the twins were also conjoined — they came as a single delivery, with their unicorn horns met in the middle.

Conjoined unicorn twins. What were the odds? About a million billion to one?

Of course, with this came the difficult decision raised with the birth of any conjoined twins: to separate or not? In some instances, usually when conjoined twins share multiple organs, the procedure is deemed too difficult and hazardous, and is dismissed, or at least delayed. But in this instance, at first glance and on the balance of probabilities, the team decided to proceed. In fact, it was the twins clearly being unicorns that concluded the matter: the crux being the horns of the dilemma. Immediately after birth, the horn was soft enough for the operation, making cauterisation possible. Later in life, with the hardening of the horn and the increase in its internal blood flow, such a procedure would become impossible. Which is not to say that at this early stage the operation was without risk. It wasn't: there was a fifty–fifty chance of success or failure. The odds were double or nothing, it would seem.

And after some delicate work with a sharp instrument and some rather deft work with some fishing line (if you've ever made a lure for fly-fishing, then you'll appreciate the handiwork involved), the operation was completed and the separation pronounced a success. Baby Y and Baby Z (as they would henceforth forever be known in medical textbooks) were, for the first time, individuals. Mother X could now nuzzle each to her bosom for them to feed. And what a splendid sight it was. The only living mother on Earth with her blessing of identical unicorn twins.

And in a simpler world that might have been where the story ended. But it proved impossible to keep such a thing a secret. Because some of those in attendance squirrelled away evidence of the event despite the non-disclosure agreements forbidding them to do so. Tissue samples. Snippets of the placenta. Ultrasound scans. EEG, ECGs … The O&G ward was looted as thoroughly as any sacred Egyptian tomb. The ill-gotten mementoes spirited away to bide their time in safe-deposit boxes and secret cupboards, like the infamous Clinton–Lewinsky blue dress. And for a time, those who had witnessed the birth were satisfied merely to keep these things hidden away as insurance against a rainy day that hopefully might never come.

But it proved impossible to keep such a miraculous thing a secret. And nor did some want to. For as global food insecurity began to rise and times became tight, those involved became restless. It was then that they realised that their precious items would only have true value if they were known about, and their provenance made public. So tongues started to wag. And, well, as we know, loose lips sink ships. Especially lips lubricated by alcohol and hunger.

And so it was that pressure began to be increasingly put on Mother X to out her rainbow brood, by those wanting to cash in on the notoriety and cash in their trinkets. Eventually Mother X could no longer ignore the dilemma she'd always hoped to avoid: to go public — or be made public? To expose — or be exposed? She could either attempt to retain some agency and control over the agenda, or be stripped of her dignity and laid bare before the eyes of global media. She chose the former.

And not since Octomom's octuplets had there been such a maternal clusterfuck.

Overnight, 'Unicorn Mom' became the top-trending story across all media, eclipsing wars, info wars, elections, scandals, everything. It wasn't possible to walk along a street, alley, hutong or passageway anywhere in the world without recognising her picture and knowing about her story.

Even so, Mother X did her best to keep the twins themselves out of the spotlight, instead offering up curated video clips and photographs to sate the demands of the public. Their exact location was a tightly guarded secret, too, and, by negotiating enough money from the deal, she was able to keep them in their own private equivalent of a witness protection programme. When the twins were older, she figured, they could decide for themselves whether to have more cosmetic surgery to further conceal their identity, and perhaps have a chance at a normal life.

In spite of all these convoluted plans and smoke and mirrors, the question remained: is it actually possible to live anonymously anymore? To disappear without leaving a trace? Or are our digital fingerprints smeared across every surface we touch? Meaning, like it or not, we will be found.

While those of a philosophical bent might be content to ponder such universal enigmas, others had their feet firmly on the ground and, far from their heads being in the clouds, had their gaze firmly fixed on the double rainbow. Curiosity about the twins was insatiable. (What did they eat? How did they play? Did they have magic powers?) And that appetite needed to be fed. With baby photos, locks of hair, and, of course, glimpses of the dear unicorns' horns.

Curiosity about Unicorn Mom was equally rapacious. And Unicorn Mom discovered the only way to get some semblance of peace was to drip-feed the monster. Soon you could buy her licensed cookbook, subscribe to her home-schooling tutorials, choose from her fashion range, and cover yourself in her perfume — which was rumoured to be an incredible aphrodisiac. She was even offered a large sum to star in adult videos, while others suggested she'd make more money by setting up an OnlyFans account — Uni-Horny Mom.

But the truth is, this was all a front. An elaborate ruse. A digital double-cross. Because the Unicorn Mom who pandered to the people was an actor. Still, people will believe what they want to believe. Such is the power of suggestion. And — just like in the satirical Japanese short story 'Dragon: The Old Potter's Tale',* where through the simple power of suggestion a whole village believed they had witnessed a black dragon ascend to heaven — everyone wanted to believe that Unicorn Mom's incredible story and life were true. And they had no reason not to.

And so, while the world was fixated on her story and the family's apparent comings and goings, the real Mother X and her unicorn babies Y and Z vanished. They headed to the world's largest and most unpopulated area: the Mongolian steppes.

Endnote

* Ryūnosuke Akutagawa, 'Dragon: The Old Potter's Tale', first appeared in *Akutagawa Ryūnosuke Zenshū* in 1919. The story is based on a 13th-century tale, and Akutagawa brings modern thinking about religion and psychology to the issue of people believing what they want to believe even when faced with facts to the contrary.

Conclusion?

It's possible that none of these stories has a conclusion of any sort. The protagonists don't have to meet, and their lives don't need to overlap. Why should they?

Life unfolds or unravels before us. That's it. To believe otherwise could be considered foolish. Loose ends don't need to tie up. There is no law in the universe that suggests they should. In fact, the opposite is almost certainly true: if entropy governs the universe, then everything tends to disorder, not order.

Therefore, we don't need to conclude anything at all.

And some people are perfectly happy with that level of ambiguity.

However, for those who do like all the pieces of the puzzle to fall into place, read on.

Entangled

Forty thousand years ago, the idea of walking with unicorns wouldn't have seemed quite as strange as it does now. Especially if you lived in Siberia. For the Siberian unicorn graced (and grazed) the plains of Eurasia at the same time as early 'modern man'. It didn't have the poise, grace or beauty that we've come to expect in our modern-day representations of unicorns for it weighed 4 tonnes, was the size of a small bus and had a horn about 3 metres long. And you would find it grazing anywhere from Kazakhstan to China. It's highly likely that it wasn't followed around by magical rainbows, for it was a beast. And a sensitive one at that. It is also suggested that one reason for its extinction was that it was a picky eater.

THIS STORY IS SET ALONG THE ROUTE OF THE
TRANS-SIBERIAN RAILWAY LINE AND ITS BRANCH
LINE THE TRANS-MONGOLIAN RAILWAY.

Tuyana-Solongo ('Radiant Rainbow') was riding on the Trans-Siberian Express, as she so often did, albeit seldom inside the carriage, as she was doing this day.

As the train rattled along, the train's conductor engaged Tuyana in conversation — which he so often never did, even if she was inside, because he'd never think even for a moment to ask her for a ticket, because she never carried one.

'I've seen another one of your kind,' he said. And let that sink in. For *she* never had.

'He was travelling the other way,' he continued. And he gesticulated over his shoulder, which meant west, as opposed to the direction they were going in, which was east.

'But he'd lost that,' he said. And nodded towards her horn.

Tuyana mulled it over. The Trans-Siberian Railway (The Great Siberian Route, to use its historical name) starts in Moscow and finishes in Vladivostok 9289 kilometres away. It crosses seven time zones and takes eight days to complete the journey. You can even travel from St Petersburg to Beijing if you take the fork at her beloved Ulan-Ude. Meaning 'he' could be anywhere by now.

When Khukhkhuu came to, it was as though his mind had been rearranged. Everything felt out of sync and out of place. A constant and monotonous *ker-chunk ker-chunk* had perhaps kept him unconscious longer than necessary, until finally the pain between his temples had grown so much that it demanded his attention. Opening his eyes, he formed the impression he was in the compartment of a train, which was odd, because he had no memory of ever boarding one. Pulling back the curtains to let in some light, he saw a featureless terrain passing by. He was thirsty. His tongue was stuck to the roof of his mouth, his head was thumping, and there was a strange chemical smell in the air. He was also bursting to have a piss. Which is when he became aware of a plastic tube sticking out of his trousers, and it suddenly dawned on him where the other end was. He tucked the tube out of sight, stood unsteadily, exited the compartment, and went in search of a toilet. Once inside he carefully removed the tubing — the make-do catheter — and relieved himself. Wiping his hands on his trousers, he checked his pockets, whereupon he realised his money was missing. Worse than that: when he looked into the mirror, he realised his horn was missing …

When he came to again it was because of a constant knocking on the lavatory door. After a pause, the lock turned, the door opened, and one of the train's conductors filled the doorframe. He took one look at Khukhkhuu and said something which can be loosely translated from the Russian as 'Get your shit together, you filthy drunk; other passengers need to use the toilet to shit, too', and closed the door.

Once back inside his compartment, with the door closed, Khukhkhuu began to think. He looked out of the window again to get his bearings.

Tuyana's mind travelled back to her recent incarceration in Ulan-Ude. There, she had met an old lag who had offered her some prison advice. 'You could sell that for a pretty penny,' he proffered. She thought he meant her ass. It was what she'd expected. To be someone's prison bitch. But he meant her horn. She decided there and then she owed him a visit.

After exchanging one form of currency — Russian roubles — for another — a carton of Peter the Great cigarettes — Tuyana headed for the jail. She went in without being handcuffed this time and queued with the other visitors. The guards fetched the old lag, who was somewhat surprised to receive a visitor. But his eyes lit up when he saw the cigarettes. And as she fed him the cigarettes, he fed her the story, and slowly but surely she got the picture. Someone with a lot of money was prepared to pay handsomely for a unicorn horn to extract the fabled alicorn inside. An aphrodisiac of the highest order. 'Put me in touch,' she said. 'I might consider selling mine … for the right price.' Here, the old lag turned coy. 'The person in question already has one,' he said. 'Not sure if they'd want another. In fact, they just got hold of one from across the border — in Mongolia.'

'Just ask, she said', dangling the final fag just out of reach.

It took a week or so, but she finally received a message.

Khukhkhuu reasoned that if he sat and waited, he would find out where he was soon enough. And as the train pulled into Krasnoyarsk, that question was answered. He was a long way from his beloved steppes. Not far on a map to be sure, but about 2000 kilometres, as the train flies, from Ulaanbaatar.

But the gap between this faraway city and his homeland was nothing to the gap now evident on his forehead. For without his horn he was like a Mongol without his horse. And stealing his horn was immeasurably worse than stealing his horse. But, again, Khukhkhuu knew he had to be patient, had to bide his time and take first things first. For he knew as surely as there was breath in his body that the punishment of whoever had stripped him of his horn would come — and would be commensurate with the crime. But first, he needed some medical attention.

Then would be time for revenge.

Meanwhile in Shaanxi, northwestern China, an archaeologist was busy at work. He was on the site of the oldest known discovery of the remains of *Elasmotherium* — the extinct genus of the Siberian unicorn. He used the softest brush to meticulously remove the fine-grained sand from the possible resting place of a once-hunted Siberian rhinoceros. It was painstaking work and took many hours, and as he did it he amused himself by thinking what he would do if he were to find and excavate a horn. The black-market value of such a thing would be enormous. And the rumour in archaeological circles was that a collector (an oligarch, no less) was dead set on reviving the species, so if DNA could be extracted from such a find he would be as rich as Croesus … And with that he once again began to use his brush to delicately and tenderly stroke the ground.

Oleg Samarkand was part-Uzbek, part-Russ, and proud son of Siberia. And while you might question his methods, there's one thing you wouldn't dare to question: his loyalty. He was pro a strong Siberia, not a subservient one. A sovereign Siberia that would have agency over its own destiny. Not one that shipped its wealth to Moscow and its sons to war (and almost certain death) in Ukraine. His fortune had been built on the exploitation of fossil fuels, and if he were to have his way now, then his future (and that of Siberia) might be built on the exploitation of his land's famous fossil remains. Bringing a species back from the dead would make a nice change from BAU (business as usual), which mainly consisted of the opposite — sending members of the human species to their grave — so the resurrection of the Siberian unicorn, extinct for 20,000 years, was his next bold plan. And right now, the Olegarch — as he'd come to be known — had a plan A and a plan B. And he was prepared to execute them both. Plan A involved DNA recovery from the fossilised remains of *Elasmotherium*, which would be brought back into existence and would once more graze the Siberian plains. Plan B involved a similar procedure, but first involved capturing the horn of a modern human-unicorn chimera — and it appeared his people had made some interesting progress in that area. They'd ambushed a Mongolian, turned a train carriage into an impromptu operating theatre and removed his horn. Left him for dead and despatched the horn to Oleg. It was now undergoing analysis.

Tuyana did some research into the murky world of trade in body parts, which in turn led her down the rabbit hole of the shadowy world of fossil trade and 'commercial' paleontology.

Only recently, the skeleton of a Tarbosaurus — the less well-known but equally ferocious cousin of the Tyrannosaurus — was unearthed in Mongolia's

Gobi Desert and was auctioned off for more than US$1 million. The Mongolian government went on record as saying: 'In Mongolia, if you find a dinosaur fossil anywhere in the country, it belongs to the people of Mongolia. If it's in America, it's there illegally.' *Wow,* Tuyana thought, *this is big business.* And started formulating bigger plans.

Khukhkhuu made his way to A&E, where he was immediately triaged to the ICU. He'd lost a lot of blood, so a transfusion was the first course of treatment prescribed, followed by liquid nitrogen cauterisation. Samples of all kinds were sent for analysis. A young female doctor checked his vital signs, and 24 hours later he was discharged: the hospital was busy and Khukhkhuu had no medical insurance.

Then, just as he was about to exit the hospital, the young doctor whispered something to him: 'If you want to find your missing horn, go and search the Onionlands.' Köke wasn't sure whether he'd heard her correctly, but nonetheless he made a mental note. She watched him leave, then the moment he was out of sight she made a call to a colleague down the line. 'I have some information I think you'd be interested in ...'

In Ulan-Ude, Tuyana had a friend who was no stranger to the dark web — a place where you buy and sell anything in complete anonymity. A digital Silk Road with one dominant religion: trade. Buyer-meet-seller-meet-buyer-meet-seller … and so it goes. In fact, 'New Silk Road' had even been the name of this dominant marketplace until it was shut down. Now trade occurred on something called Alpha Bay.

Tuyana and her friend located the market for unusual body parts and set to work. They found the post relating to the sale of a severed unicorn horn almost immediately, and placed a bid on that. Let's just say that among all the things listed for sale — and they certainly made the mind boggle — a severed unicorn horn didn't even seem that remarkable. Next, firmly putting their boggling minds back on-task, they created a post listing Tuyana's intact horn for sale and posted that. The fuse was lit.

[Excerpt: The Body Part Bazaar]

Requests to buy organs are fairly common on the dark web, often made by desperate patients on waiting lists who fear they won't live long enough to get the organ they need the legal way. The World Health Organization estimates that there are roughly 10,000 illegal organ transplant surgeries per year. Unsurprisingly, the more vital the organ, the more

it costs. A human heart or liver runs
between $100,000 and $200,000, while
a functioning set of eyes costs closer to
$1,200.
The creepier part, though, is that the market
for illicit body parts is much bigger than
that for necessary, transplantable organs.
In fact, non-transplantable parts like hands,
feet and forearms tend to be the best deal,
each running for less than $500 apiece.
(It's probably best not to think about why
someone would want to buy them.)

After leaving the hospital, Khukhkhuu stopped people at random, asked whether they knew where 'the onionlands' were and if they could possibly show him the way. Most ignored him, and some crossed the street to avoid him, but one person pointed to an internet café and suggested he ask inside there. So he did. And, even though Köke had no money, the kindly owner of the café let him go online, and even showed him where 'the onionlands' were. Khukhkhuu's immediate education involved the discovery that 'the onionlands' was slang for places on the dark web you could visit via the TOR network. (TOR stands for 'The Onion Router', which alludes to the way it functions: using the TOR browser is like peeling back the layers of the internet to reveal its dark heart.) And suddenly, everything became clear. He was a pawn in a bigger game. He was merchandise in a market that until this very moment he hadn't even known existed. He now also knew he needed to get home. He was going to need his horse. And his bow.

Oleg was masterminding his own business when he got a message: 'a live one' had come on the market, and was he interested? He told his people to keep an eye on it; he was interested. If they could extract the alicorn from it, he'd be a billionaire twice over.

It wasn't too long after that when he got another message, this time about the Mongolian, and it provided a chance to tie up a loose end. *Eto dolzhen byt moy schastlivyy den*, he thought. *This must be my lucky day.*

Tuyana needed to work out an appropriate meeting point. It had to be either hidden in plain sight, or somewhere so obvious a gathering wouldn't warrant a second look. Both trades would have to occur simultaneously. In truth, her only aim was to retrieve the severed unicorn horn. Later, she would find its owner and repatriate it. She had no intention of losing her own: using it as bait was a high-risk strategy, but she had an ace up her sleeve.

Meanwhile in Shaanxi, the archaeologist was tumescent. He was beginning to think (nay, believe) that he might be on the brink of revealing the jawbone of an *Elasmotherium* — the Siberian unicorn — which might in turn lead to a full skull, which might then lead to … Here, he could barely contain himself — he practically ejaculated. After regaining his composure, he wrangled some interns to do the delicate, painstaking and somewhat tedious chore of an infinitesimally slow reveal, while he himself took off to quickly research the going price for such a find (and also beat himself off in the portacabins while scrolling through archaeologist dating sites). Not content with carbon-dating, there's also a thriving scene in dating archaeologists. If this sounds like it's stretching the bounds of possibility, then visit the link in the footnotes and be enlightened.

It has also been noted, in surveys about the professions most likely to be replaced by AI (artificial intelligence), that archaeology ranks bottom — the least likely to be replaced by AI. It is somewhat ironic that one of the world's oldest professions is, to some degree, future-proof. So why not bag an anthropologist while you can?

Now back in Karakorum, 'little' Khukhkhuu's homecoming was no quiet affair. The return of the prodigal Uni-Khan had been foretold, and much mare's milk was consumed as he told the story of how he came to lose his blessed horn, that a black market existed for such things, and how he was determined to reclaim it. Fired up by righteous outrage, and fomented by fermented mare's milk, the tribe swore to enact the most horrible revenge on the perpetrators.

Some people assert that the art of strategy is imposing the time, location and conditions for battle upon the enemy. With that in mind, Tuyana set the time, date and location of the meeting and sent this to the buyer on Alpha Bay. Then she packed her bags, and, along with her hacker friend, prepared to head south. She had chosen a site across the border in Mongolia. A place near Ulaanbaatar. She hoped this would surface the Mongolian.

The Oleg-arch received news from his minions. He hadn't been south for a while, but a short stay in Ulaanbaatar could be fun. He could check in on his vassals there.

In Shaanxi, the ground shook. Not because of an earthquake, but because all of the archaeologist's dreams had come true. The endeavours of the interns had revealed the wholly intact form of the horn of a Siberian unicorn. 'O frabjous day! Callooh! Callay!' he shouted as he leapt up and down. The interns just looked at him askance. Boomers sure have a strange lingo. It's one of the quirks of dating them.

In Karakorum, Khukhkhuu paid a visit to the village's IT support, which might sound a little bizarre — but that's progress. Many Mongolians might still live in traditional gers (or yurts) with floors made from heavy, woven carpets, but that doesn't mean they don't have 21st-century mod cons such as satellite TV and mobile internet. He located IT nested in the ger next to the shaman's, and together Köke and the IT guy looked in on Alpha Bay — the New Silk Road — and found exactly what they were looking for. The next morning a raiding party assembled, saddled up, and with one voice summoned the spirit of the immortal Chinggis as they cried: '*We ride!*'

The archaeologist documented the find, then instructed his team to secure the site. Barely had the orders left his lips, and he was high-tailing it to the airport. Chatter on the *new* Silk Road (aka Alpha Bay) had it that a big meet-up was about to take place near Ulaanbaatar — *and* the world's foremost collector of unicorn horns would be there. Therefore, he needed to be there, too.

It was still dark when Tuyana's vehicle pulled up at a crossroads about 50 kilometres east of Ulaanbaatar. They were the first to location (as far as she could tell). She stood in the middle of the crossroads and waited, her shadow (and that of her horn) acting as a moon-dial. As the sky softened, they'd have an uninterrupted view for miles. She was live bait. And it was almost time.

Everything was quiet, but then a low thrum signalled many engines approaching. Gradually, Tuyana could make out the dark outline of a fleet of vehicles on the horizon — Toyota Land Cruisers by the throaty sound of them. And, cast into somewhat conspicuous relief at the end of the black cavalcade, a white ambulance.

As the fleet got to within 50 metres of her, it paused. But the white ambulance kept moving forward until it was at the head of the column. And it kept on moving straight towards the crossroads, overshooting it by a few metres (deliberately, by the look of things) before coming to a stop with its rear doors facing Tuyana. Against the backdrop of the surrounding purring engines, slowly the rear doors opened.

The ambulance's internal light lit up the team of medical staff waiting inside. One of them stepped down from the ambulance and walked forward, carrying a white medical-grade chiller box. Placed the chiller box on the ground, and opened it, tilting the box forward slightly, to display its cargo, which was wrapped in clear plastic, resting on ice, and surrounded by waves of dry ice. Tuyana knew exactly what it was: a recently severed unicorn horn. She bent down and picked it up.

The medic lowered her surgical mask — it was the doctor from the Krasnoyarsk hospital (although Tuyana would not know this) — and was about to speak when all of sudden a Russian-accented male voice spoke first: 'A horn for a horn.'

Tuyana jumped. Distracted by the sickening yet mesmerising sight of the severed horn, she had dropped her guard.

A tall man stood at three o' clock from the chiller. It was the Oleg-arch. He continued: 'When you're ready, we're ready for you ...' — and gestured towards the back of the ambulance where the medical team waited. The inference was clear.

Tuyana bit back her fear and spoke up: 'And my fee?'

Oleg waved a hand, and a vassal walked forward with a canvas bag, placed it on the floor, and unzipped it to reveal its contents: banknotes. 'Of course ... a mere formality,' said Oleg smoothly.

At that moment, a rasping sound like the buzzing of a fly got louder and louder. It was paired with a single spotlight veering left and right like a drunken sun (or for that matter, a drunken moon — it probably depends upon the culture you're brought up in). It got louder and louder and brighter and brighter until it screeched to a halt. A motorbike had just gate-crashed the party.

A passenger leapt off the back of the bike, and ran forward, shouting: 'Wait! Wait!' It was the archaeologist. 'I have a unicorn horn!' Tuyana, Oleg and the doctor all looked at the intruder. Then at each other, then back to the intruder. They spoke in unison: 'So do I.'

Hmmm. Looks like we've got ourselves a standoff …

Suddenly, the vacuum of the stand-off found itself the epicentre of a barrage of pyrotechnics. Fireballs tore through the crossroads — incoming from four directions. Screaming, ululations, the clatter of hooves. Noise, fire, chaos, Sturm und Drang. Then silence.

The dust gradually settled to reveal that the shocked attendees now numbered three, not four. Still present were the doctor, the Oleg-arch and the archaeologist. Tuyana was nowhere to be seen. And nor was the severed unicorn horn.

Tuyana, herself, was stunned. One minute she had been standing at a crossroads holding a severed unicorn horn. The next moment, and in a single move, she'd been picked up off the ground and thrown across the saddle of a horse moving at breakneck speed by its rider, who displayed an agility and command of his steed that could only come from someone who'd practically been born in the saddle.

They weren't alone either. She was flanked by horses galloping just as fast and ridden by other fearsome-looking warriors. What also stood out — and would remain imprinted in her memory forever — was the smell of burning hair. The horses' manes had been set alight. Some were still burning. Others were now just smoking. A traditional Mongolian tactic of shock and awe. It had been used to bring terror to the steppe in the Middle Ages, and it was clearly just as effective now.

As the horde thundered on, Tuyana stole a glance up at her — captor? saviour? — and became aware that the horn she was still clutching had once belonged to the rider who was now holding her fast. It was a perfect match for the scar on his forehead. Khukhkhuu had found his horn. She had found a brother.

Khukhkhuu and his clan had watched from afar before slowly closing in. They lit the horses' manes so that the wild horses without riders bolted forward in terror and ran amok through the assembled fleet of trucks, causing chaos. That was the moment for Khukhkhuu and his *alps* (warriors) to strike. And no one could match their speed or agility. The woman at the centre of the crossroads — who was clearly the centre of attention, and was in possession of his precious and severed unicorn horn — also had a horn of her own still attached to her forehead. He hadn't foreseen that particular detail, but it was something that could be examined later. For now, he picked his line and struck like a lightning bolt. It was all over in a matter of milliseconds. And now he had his horn back, albeit in a plastic bag, and he also had a unicorn over his saddle. Strange days indeed.

Back at the crossroads, matters hadn't yet come to a close, but they soon would. The Mongolian riders had created a circle around those present and that circle was now slowly constricting, squeezing its inhabitants in a chokehold. Outside that circle was a ring of police vehicles. The police were keen to interview each attendee, and it wouldn't be long before Oleg, the doctor and the archaeologist would be helping them with their enquiries. There was a whole list of topics the police were keen to discuss, including kidnapping, theft, racketeering, and the illegal trafficking of body parts and fossils. And there was all the time in the world to do so. Time moved differently here.

Dawn was breaking, and as the first shafts of daylight burst over the horizon, any tall objects would catch the light first. At this early hour, and standing tall at 40 metres, there was only one object being lit: the enormous monument of Chinggis Khan built only a hundred metres or so from the crossroads. The location deliberately chosen by Tuyana. First the Emperor's head was bathed in gold, then the light slowly descended, revealing every glorious detail cast in stainless steel of the rider astride his horse. It took a full minute, and the effect was pure Hollywood. Exit night. Enter light. And there wasn't a person present who would ever forget how small it made them feel.

Now safely back in Karakorum, Khukhkhuu and Tuyana were received like conquering heroes returning with their spoils. Justice had been served. The clan had their precious son back. And their status had been restored. The severed horn would once again be a totem and a beacon for all those that believed in its divine status.

To return to the question posed at the very start of these stories: Is it a blessing to be born a unicorn? It's impossible to say. But it was a blessing that these two unicorns now had each other, because for the very first time in their lives they were not alone.

Later, Khukhkhuu returned Tuyana to the railway station in Ulaanbaatar so that she could begin her journey home — first to Ulan-Ude, then to Lake Baikal.

The Trans-Mongolian Express pulled into the station and its passengers prepared to disembark. As they did so, Tuyana couldn't help but notice a mother struggling with two infants, so she began to help them safely down from the carriage to the platform. In the kerfuffle one of the children lost a hat. Tuyana recovered it and went to put it back on the child's head. In that instant, Tuyana saw a protuberance on the child's forehead which the hat had been covering. She looked at the twins' mother, who looked back at her, and a knowing glance passed between the two. It was Mother X with Baby Y and Baby Z. And they had just met Tuyana-Solongo ('Radiant Rainbow').

Denouement

Now back at Lake Baikal, Tuyana replayed the series of extraordinary events in her mind so she could process them. It had been a most unusual time. She was down by the lake's shore and it was frozen over. In such weather, locals would come down to the lake and cut a hole in the inch-thick ice so that they could fish. And nearby was a spot where someone had done exactly that. As she pondered things the water began to ripple and a pointed object began to emerge from it. And kept rising. It had a spiral design and got thicker the more it rose. After about a metre of this, the beginnings of a head appeared. She wondered if she was looking at a species not unlike a narwhal, which would have been unique even for Baikal, with its unique seal population.

(Stranger things had been spotted.) But then the head revealed itself and it had a thick skin and bulging eyes. Which in turn revealed themselves to be neoprene and a diving mask. The creature pulled itself from the water and onto the ice. Then stood, removed its oxygen tanks, and unzipped its skin. Long flowing tresses of hair fell to its shoulders. The creature removed its diving mask leaving its outline imprinted into its skin. It was gorgeous. And it began to speak.

And in an accent Tuyana didn't recognise, it said: '*Allow me to introduce myself … my name is Navi. I heard about your adventures, and figured you might need a friend …*'

TO BE CONTINUED

Footnotes

The weird commerce of the dark web:
https://www.pymnts.com/news/retail/2020/the-weird-commerce-of-the-dark-web/

The body bazaar:
https://pubmed.ncbi.nlm.nih.gov/11936152/

Dating archaeologists:
https://medium.com/cultural-resource-management/how-to-date-an-archaeologist-d8b1c274d918

Author AMA (ask me anything)

Why the steppes?

Through no wish or fault of their own, the author was born in England at the latter end of the 20th century. Which is a long way from the old Silk Road, the trans-Siberian railway, and the Mongolian steppe, all of which feature strongly in these stories. So why would the author choose to place them in such far-flung places?

Firstly, the premise demanded it. There should be no rhyme nor reason to the location of a supposed *one-in-a-billion* birth. No expectation, no assumption, and no bias. Spin the globe and throw a dart at it.

Secondly, the author didn't want to write about people or places that were too familiar. They wanted to cover new ground. Distance from the subject matter was important.

Thirdly, the stories themselves demanded it. There is a point in the writing process where what you set out to do, isn't what eventuates. The stories themselves and the needs of their protagonists take over. They begin to write their own stories.

However, the author did want to place the stories in such a way that they had reasons for being. Reasons that could be cultural, allegorical, historical, geographical, or artful. The narwhal being the 'unicorn of the sea'; the steppes being the oldest known birthplace of human-horse partnership; the uniqueness of the rainbow mountain formations in China; the Mongolian people and their consummate equestrian skill. These are things that allow a story to be bedded down in a believable way. Having 'truth to the story' helps strengthen the fiction.

Then, there is an ancestral answer. These days, we have the tools to trace the roots of our DNA. The National Geographic Genographic Project is an example of one such experimental project. According to that, the author's haplogroup is classified as R1b1b2a1a4... This string of letters and numbers identifies a specific genetic mutation in the human genome that the author carries in his DNA. The mutation itself tells you where on the human family tree a group of people branched off from the others and went their own way. (The R1b1 nomenclature is for the paternal migration, the father's gene. Mitochondrial gene analysis, on the other hand, is the journey of a mother's DNA.)

The exodus of humankind from Africa forms the main trunk of the tree with all its other limbs branching out from that. Branches of the tree head in all directions north, east, south and west and different branches carry different mutations. The genetic mutations you carry are the coordinates (geographical and chronological) needed to place you on the tree.

As it turns out, the author's ancestors came out of Africa and headed north through Persia to Turkmenistan, then to Kazakhstan before making a sharp left and heading for Europe.

Kazakhstan is the near eastern end of the steppes. The author was aware of this when placing the final story and because of that Kazakhstan nearly became a key location in it, but the route of the Trans-Siberian railway proved a more decisive storytelling device.

Kazakhstan, then, was out. Ulaanbaatar was in.

Lastly, serendipity. A visit to a nearby Lilliput Library and a fortuitous encounter with the library angel meant a thumbed copy of *On the Trail of Genghis Khan* came into the author's possession. This lit the flame for the region, which was further fanned when the author threw himself into 'The Mongol Empire' by Craig Benjamin, a 24-episode lecture series and historical epic provided by The Great Courses.

Scottish people are yoo-ni-korns

A rather unusual fact unearthed during the writing process is that a unicorn forms part of the coat of arms of Scotland. Quite why no one seems to know (there are several competing explanations). The English had a lion on theirs, and Scottish one-upmanship decreed a unicorn would henceforth be their own iconic mascot. In a not dissimilar way, no one really knows why a series of medieval unicorn tapestries has been a fixture of the walls of Stirling Castle since the 1500s — but they were mentioned in the royal record of inventory at that time.

A similar revelation is that Cunninghams also are unicorns — a unicorn gracing this family's coat of arms too. Which dovetails sweetly with the author's Irish mother Elizabeth Cunningham being one such blessed creature. She was beautiful, enchanting, and had a long mane of thick hair, and therefore fits the bill nicely.

Network effects

It's one thing to write about places one's never been and of cultures one's never seen (in fact, it's liberating), but should one's thoughts ever go out into the world and take on a life of their own, it's only fair to them that they've been stress-tested against real world demons lest they should find themselves in the way of harm. With that in mind, the author set about finding advance readers in (or from) Greenland, China, Mongolia and Siberia. (Surely, thanks to 21st-century connectedness — Facebook's social graph or LinkedIn's network effects — they'd know someone who knew someone … it's a small world after all. And happily, it worked out that way.)

Some people are vectors of connection. In this instance, Calle Sjoenel and Calvin Soh were vital. Calle (based in Stockholm) was a gateway to people in Denmark who in turn were close to people with a more intimate knowledge of Greenland. Calle connected me to Rasmus Hogdall, who was kind enough to introduce me to Danish author René Toft.

Calvin was like an arrow whose trajectory ranged as far as Ulaanbaatar in Mongolia, reaching Crystal Naran (Bolor Narantsatsralt), who became my first ever Mongolian friend.

Crystal then performed Mongolian magic of her own. First with the script, and second, by introducing me to my first Siberian friend, Alexander Sedov, who lives and works between Omsk and Sakhalin, which means he travels practically the same route of the Trans-Siberian railway as described in the book. Alexander will be visiting Lake Baikal soon and his report on the nightlife of Ulan-Ude was so brilliant I used it in its entirety.

Lastly, a happy encounter with a Kiwi friend in my own street brought me rather unexpectedly to my second Siberian friend. I bumped into Guy Hamling quite by accident one afternoon and our conversation about Iranian freedom and NZ-based Radio FarsiLand led to a conversation about a desire to travel to Mongolia and Siberia, which is when Guy mentioned his friend Sarafima Fatkulina who's currently living in Auckland but from the Barnaul region of the Altai mountains in Siberia. How about that? You scour the world for help only to find an answer in your own street.

Coffee with mattak *(whale skin and blubber)*

Where there's coffee, there's conversation (and perhaps even yoo-ni-korns). As an habitué of the Postal Service café in Grey Lynn, Auckland, and a devotee of the Kokako coffee they serve there, I'm friends with all the baristas. Postal Service's front-of-house team was recently bolstered by the arrival of a young Scottish traveller/surfer by the name of Nicole Linton, and Nicole soon became pivotal in the story behind these stories. Not only did she become a sounding board, an advance reader, and spokesperson for her generation, but a previous paramour of hers not only had knowledge of Greenland, they were in Greenland. And that's how Steffen Neilsen came into the fold and was able to read the chapter set in Disko Bugten, Greenland, while actually being present in Disko Bugten, Greenland.

Another Dane, author René Toft, introduced me to the Greenlandic custom of adding *mattak* to hot coffee as a replacement for sugar so the fat melts and it becomes quite a special drink. A detail I just had to add.

Queer yoo-ni-korns

I wanted to avoid — at all costs — a hetero-normative telling of this story and looked to people with greater knowledge of and closer connection to the full spectrum of 21st-century identity than I might have. Anna Boivin, student counsellor at MDS (Media Design School), was a great ally and provided great insight into how a young person's view of their own identity might be ambiguous, in flux, or hard to pin down. Just like the situation Tuyana-Solongo finds herself in.

***Making the yoo-ni-korn with two backs/The
intriguing details of a yoo-ni-korn's sex life***

Joanna Woutersz was curious enough to suggest the following idea: *'Can you explore sexuality from Tuyana's perspective? Perhaps an exploration of pleasure that is not bound by body or at least the way that body is generally referred to?'* And I think that's an excellent theme to explore in *Yoo-ni-korn* book two and a great place to end here.

In praise of
Yoo-ni-korn

'I love the lyrical writing, the rhythm, the mythology, the intertwining of history and myth. It was a ride — away from reality.'

Joanna Woutersz, Corporate PR executive,
Australian yoo-ni-korn

Yoo-ni-korn transported me in the way that the best magical fiction does — to another land, but one that also calls for reflection on identity, belonging and that eternal question — who are we? I loved the lyrical descriptions, the fantasy and the way that Andy Blood weaves legend, myth and visions into a story that crosses cultures and landscapes.'

Joanna Woutersz, Corporate PR executive,
Australian yoo-ni-korn

'Nothing brings back childhood memory like reading the story of Bai Longma. This chapter was a wonder, fun to read, and painted amazing visuals for me. From seeing the message in the envelope "By a pomegranate tree ringed by a fence in a field of flowers, you will find your answer" to finding the "The Unicorn in Captivity" painting was like a game play with treasure hunting map. So much fun! I think it is genius … all the stories somehow all lead to one mysterious place.'

Lola Luo, creative person, Chinese yoo-ni-korn

'*Yoo-ni-korn* is a story of wonder, danger and mystery — it is the world as we know it but entwined with magic. It is at once an exploration and celebration of identity – a true "blessing" to read.'

Nicole Linton, Master of Arts and Master of Science, surfer, Scottish yoo-ni-korn

'*Yoo-ni-korn* is a fantasy brought to life, a brief history of the world with splendid visuals and legendary lore.'

Lola Luo, creative person, Chinese yoo-ni-korn

'*Yoo-ni-korn* has a great way of combining what are perhaps unbelievable events made not only believable but recognisable to the unicorns amongst us.'

Anna Boivin, counsellor, pool-shark, Kiwi yoo-ni-korn

'I was impressed by Andy's knowledge of Siberia and its culture. Several times I had a smile on my face, especially about Lenin, about milk vodka. And about archaeologists.'

Serafima Fatkulina, Altai yoo-ni-korn

'The reading was really surprising and unusual for me. Having two small and active kids have lack time to read. And mostly concentrated on fairy tales, comics and my favourite documentary and historical readings. This novel took me from the first story. For me it was a new or well forgotten genre. I had no clue what will be the end. Read in one breath.'

Alexander Sedov, Siberian yoo-ni-korn

'For. Fuck's. Sake. I am so sorry. I completely forgot. I was stuck with too much on my plate and forgot to get back to you. I even read it and really enjoyed it. I just forgot to write back. I hope it is not too late.'

René Toft, author, Danish yoo-ni-korn

Also by the author

Non-fiction

Full Bleed

Full Bleed — 1st Anniversary Edition

Fiction

Near Futures. Far-Fetched. Volume 1.

Near Futures. Far-Fetched. Volume 2.

Acknowledgements

Yoo-ni-korn is proudly one hundred per cent human made. In fact, the same group of incredible carbon-based lifeforms that made my first four books have made this* one too. Finlay Macdonald, Kate Stone, Cheryl Smith, Eva Chan and Nic Neame. If only I could clone you.

The marketing, however, that's another story. The yoo-ni-korns featured in print, video and online media were made using Open AI's Dall-E software. Those that spoke were brought to life using D-ID's Creative Reality studio. Though all their scripts were written by me.

The marked difference in the making of *Yoo-ni-korn* versus my previous creations, however, was the magnitude of the involvement of other people. People whose cultures I knew next to nothing about beyond the education I was able to get from trusted sources such as 'The Mongol Empire' by Professor Craig Benjamin for The Great Courses.*

I am fortunate indeed that the following people became my guides, my collaborators, my interpreters, trusted lieutenants, confidants, and friends: Joanna Woutersz (Australia), Nicole Linton (Scotland), Lola Luo (China), Anna Boivin (New Zealand), Crystal Naran (Bolor Narantsatsralt) (Mongolia), Serafima Fatkulina (Altai, Siberia), Alexander Sedov (Siberia), René Toft (Denmark), Steffen Neilsen (Greenland).

Making *Yoo-ni-korn* has opened my eyes and expanded my horizons. I feel blessed.

Footnote

* Twenty-four half-hour lectures delivered by award-winning teacher and historian Craig Benjamin of Grand Valley State University. Explore the paradox of the Mongols' extreme barbarity combined with their enlightened religious attitudes and respect for high civilisation ...

About the author

Andy Blood has spent three decades at the forefront of advertising and technology, working across the globe for some of the world's best ad agencies and biggest global brands. He was the world's most-awarded executive creative director 2016–17, and holds three Cannes Grand Prix, a case of Pencils from D&AD (Design and Art Direction), and a trove of metal from the major international creative award shows.

On his watch and under his direction, the blood of the All Blacks was used in the making of a special-edition poster, ads were run on the national currency and inside actual passports, and the by-product of the brewing process was used to make a biofuel that was sold nationwide.

Uniquely, he spent five years at Facebook Creative Shop, where he was proud to receive an executive producer credit for the documentary *Losing Lena*, which investigated the subject of gender bias in technology.

He is an identical twin who was raised in the spa town of Buxton in Derbyshire ('Aquae Arnemetiae' in

Roman times). His father was a virtuoso guitarist who spent the 1970s touring US Army bases in Germany playing Jimi Hendrix covers. His mother was a Playboy Bunny.

His ancestor Colonel Thomas Blood was an Irish mercenary who stole the Crown Jewels of England in 1671.

If ideas are a product of their environment, then his background is about as fertile as you can get.

@thebloodster

Printed in Great Britain
by Amazon

26668382R00045